W9-CCG-343

First published in Switzerland under the title *Luis' Raumfahrt*.

First published in the United States, Great Britain, Canada, Australia, and New Zealand in 2005 by North-South Books, an imprint of NordSüd Verlag AG, Gossau Zürich, Switzerland

Distributed in the United States by North-South Books Inc., New York.
Library of Congress Cataloging-in-Publication Data is available.
A CIP catalogue record for this book is available from The British Library.
ISBN 0-7358-2007-4 (trade edition) 10 9 8 7 6 5 4 3 2 1

Printed in Italy

Anna Aphid

By Christine Goppel

North-South Books
New York / London

Once there was a little aphid named Anna.

Anna lived on a big green leaf with her aphid papa, her aphid mama, and all her aphid siblings.

One day, Anna asked an odd question: "Papa, what is there beyond those leaves?"

"There are more leaves, of course, where more aphids live," answered her father, who on account of his age was considered to be quite wise.

"How do you know that?" Anna asked.

"I don't know for certain, but it is very likely."

"But I want to know for sure," Anna said.

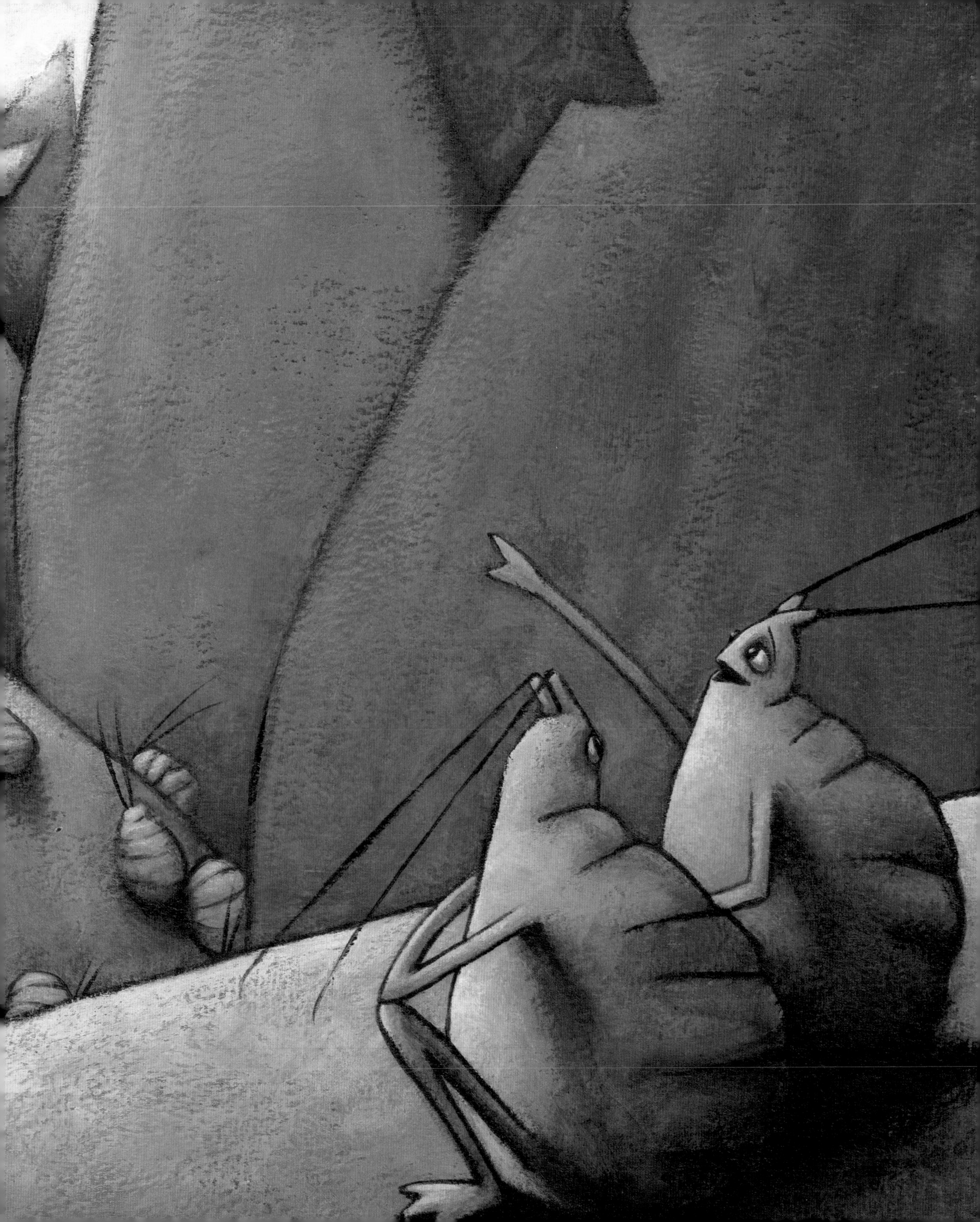

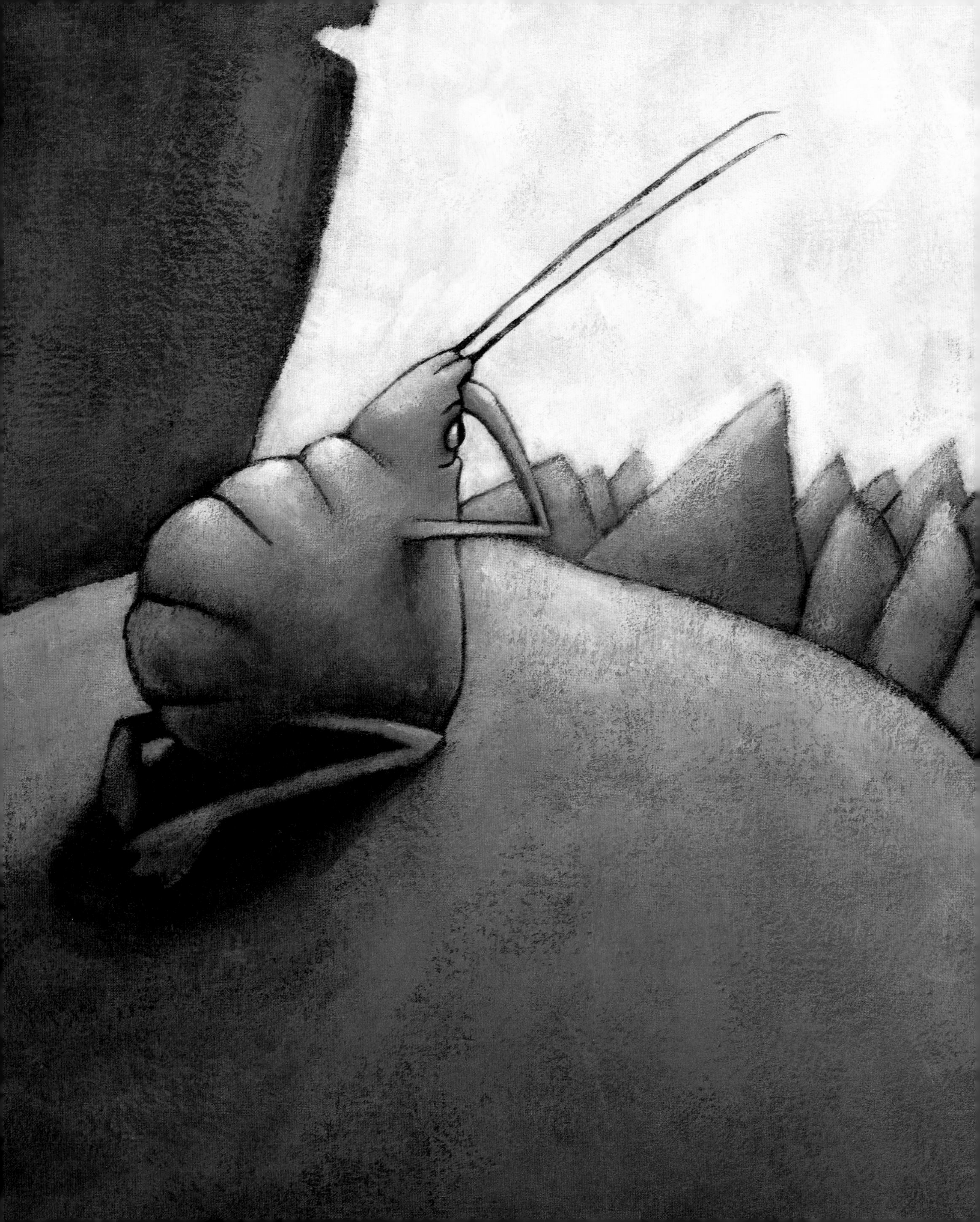

So Anna set off to find out.

And what did she find beyond those leaves?

More leaves, of course, where more aphids lived. And beyond those leaves were many more leaves, where many more aphids lived.

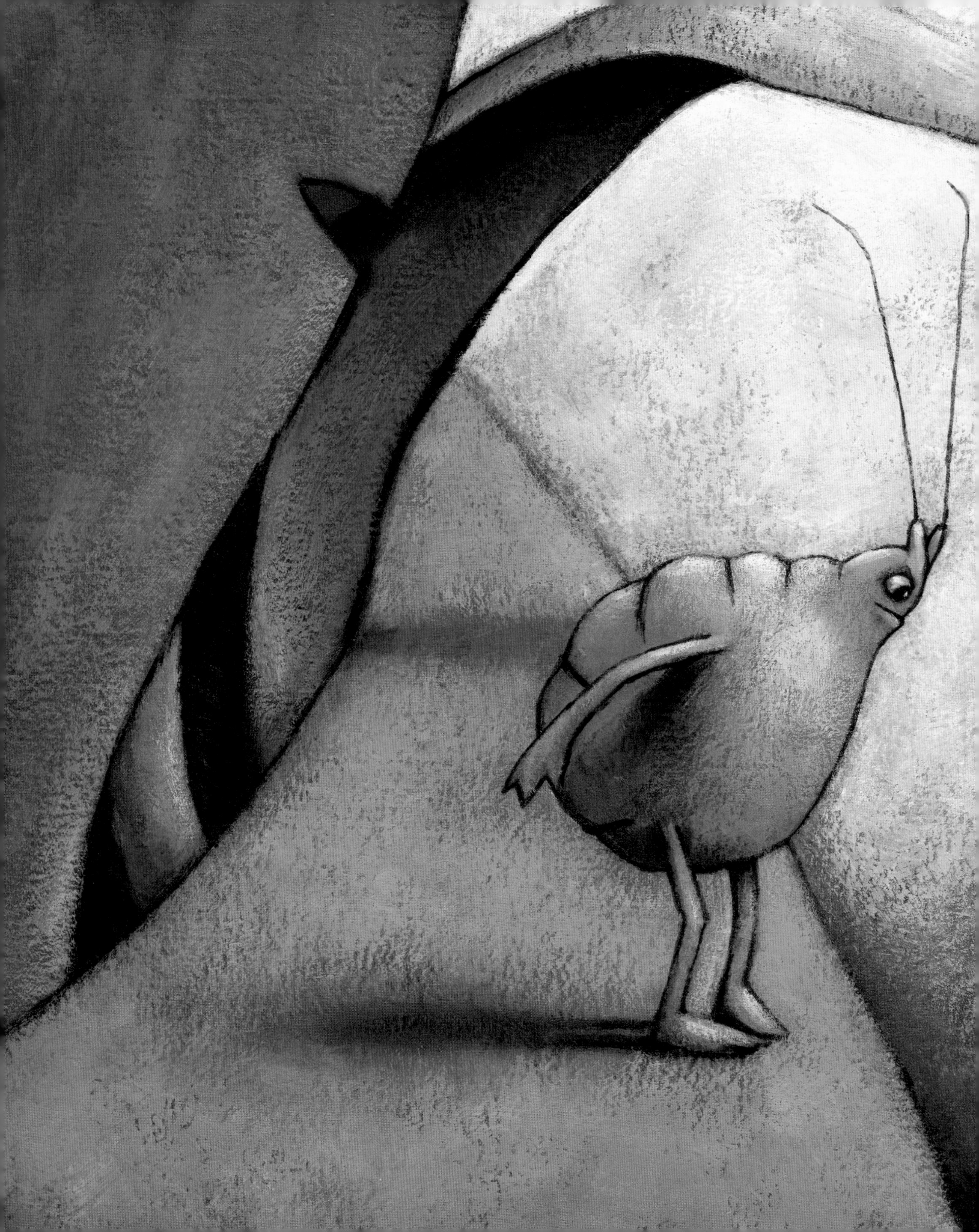

Anna thought that this would go on forever, when suddenly she passed the last leaf. She stood at the edge. There was nothing more as far as she could see.

"Was that the end of the world?" she asked her father when she returned home.

"I would think so," her father replied. "At least, it is very likely."

"I want to know for sure," Anna said. "I will go and see if something exists beyond the edge."

"You can't do that!" cried her father. "You could fall off the edge and never be seen or heard from again."

Anna was very disappointed.

But that night she had a dream. In the dream, she had wings and could fly out over the edge of the world.

When Anna awoke the next morning, an amazing thing had happened: she had actually grown a pair of wings!

How lucky was that!

Anna immediately began to try them.

It didn't take long before she could fly quite well. She flew so well that she decided she would risk an attempt at the edge of the world.

“Good-bye, Papa. Good-bye, Mama. Good-bye, little brothers and sisters!” cried Anna. She spread her wings and sailed off over the edge as if there were nothing to it.

She flew at aphid speed, which is just as fast as an aphid can go. She flew out into space. The universe was gigantic.

For a long time there was nothing at all. Then she came near the sun. It was unbelievably bright and unbearably hot.

Landing impossible, thought Anna.

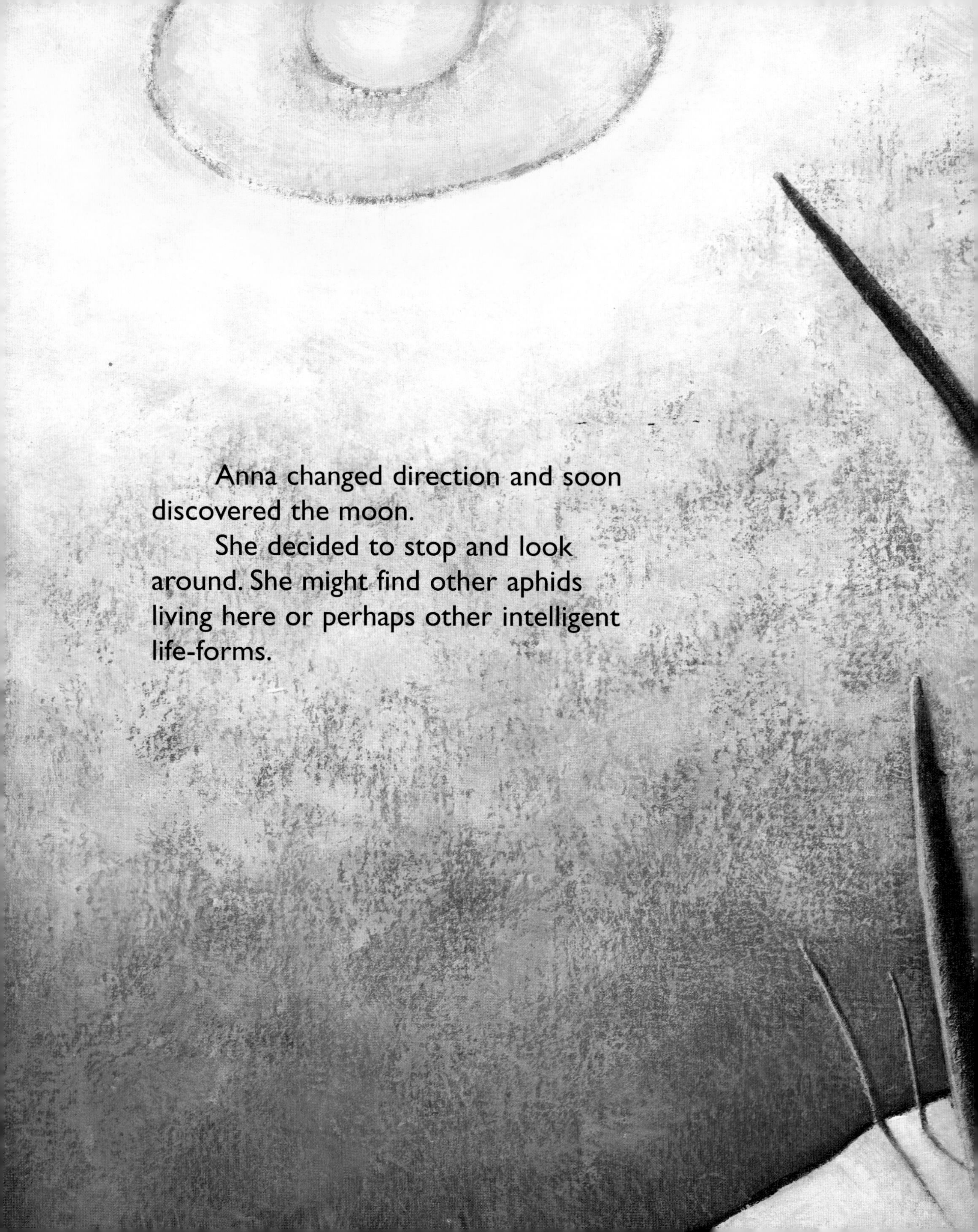

Anna changed direction and soon discovered the moon.

She decided to stop and look around. She might find other aphids living here or perhaps other intelligent life-forms.

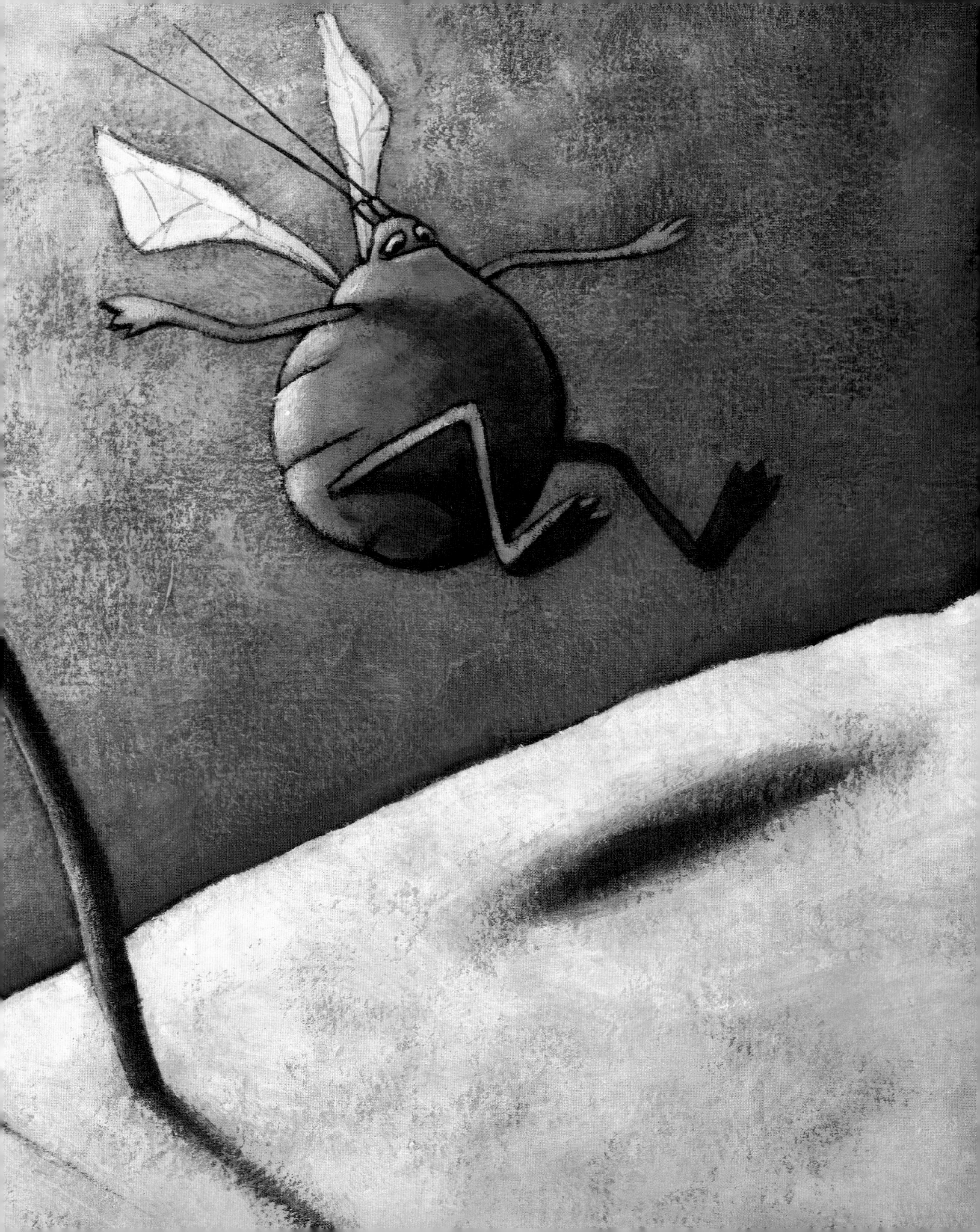

The surface of the moon was quite different from her home planet. Something strange was growing here that certainly wasn't a leaf. Perhaps it was edible?

No. It tasted terrible. No wonder no aphids lived here.

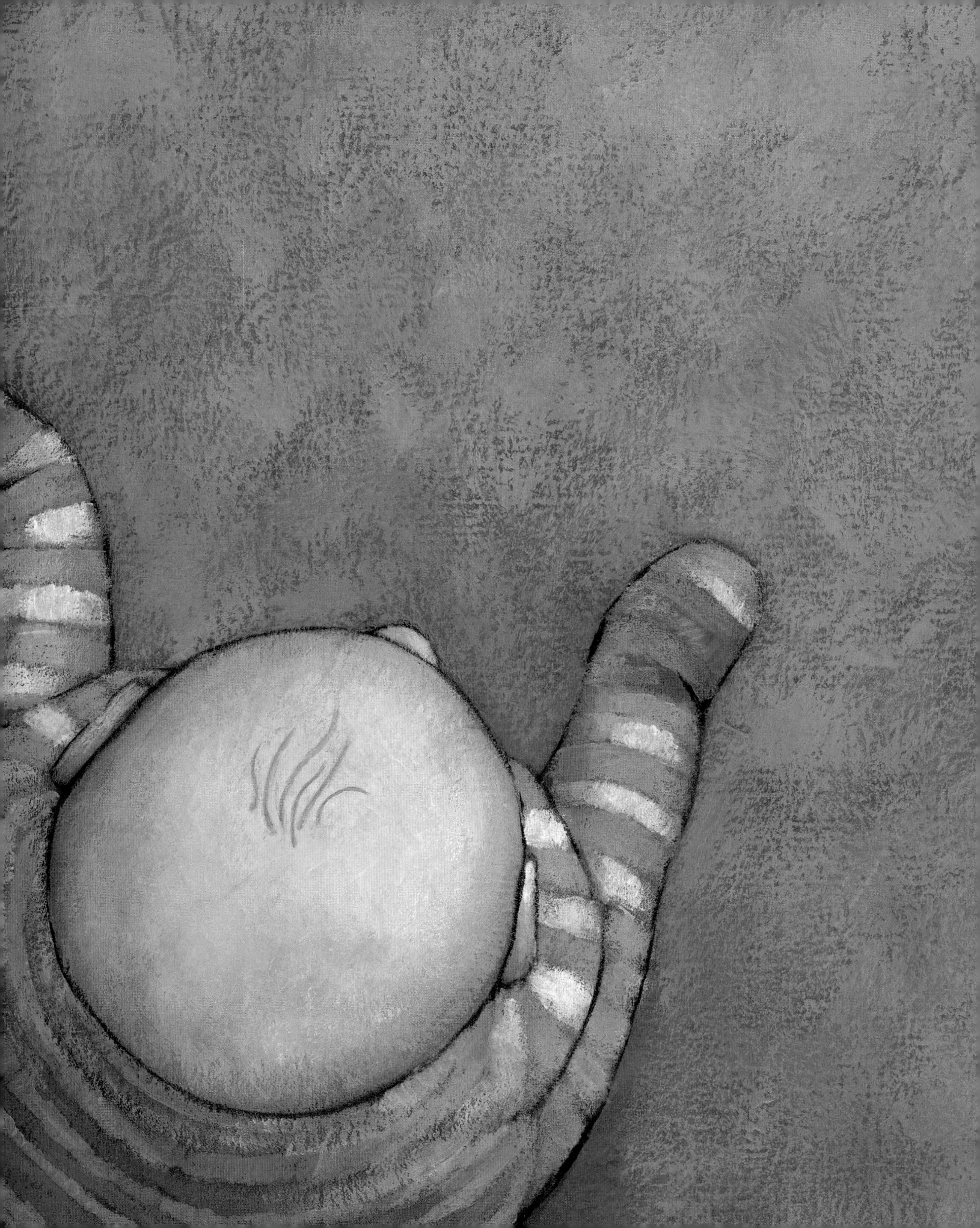

There wasn't much more to discover on the moon, so Anna flew on. Soon she encountered a stream of comets soaring through the universe.

When one flew close to Anna, she grabbed it and held on tight.

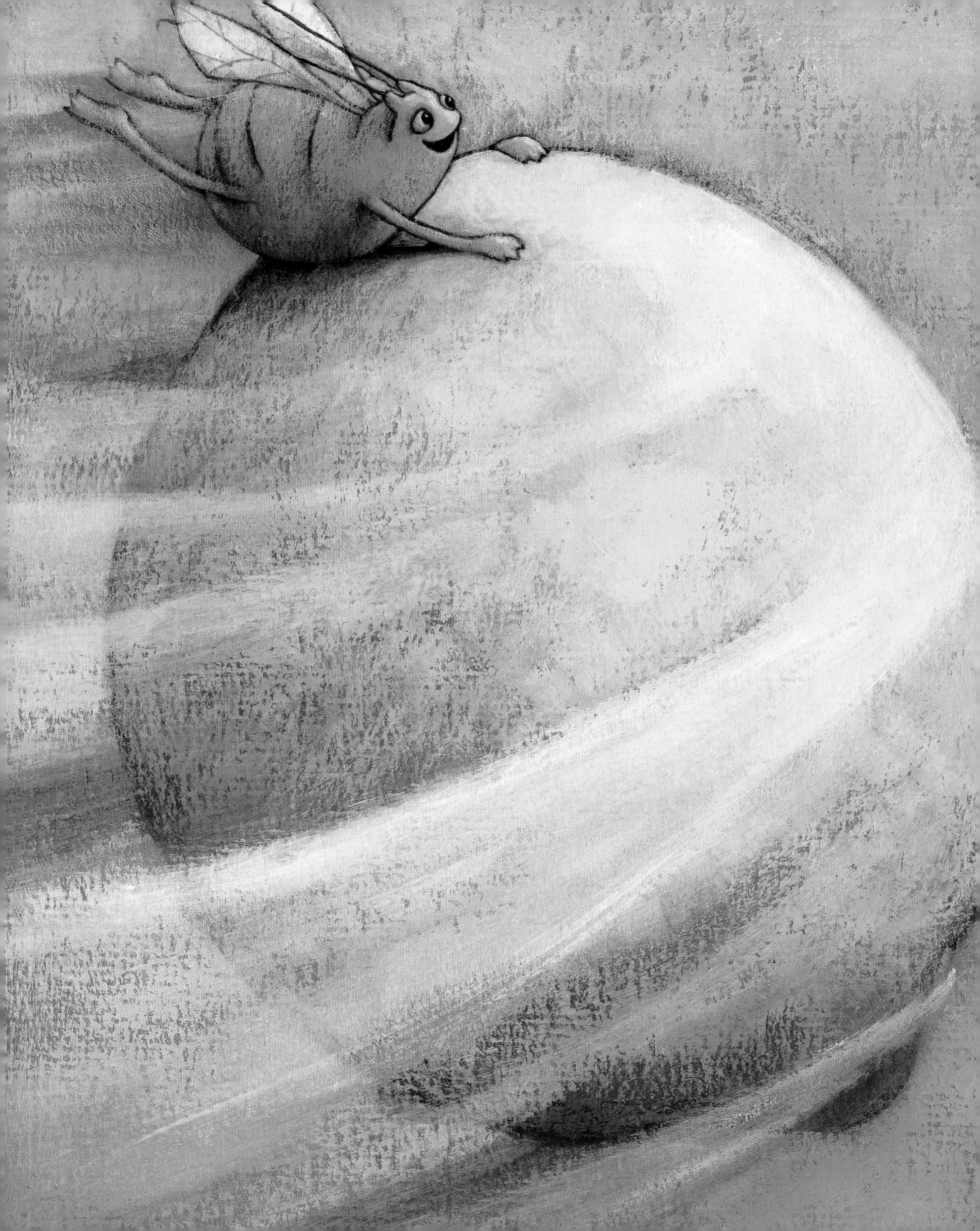

Zooming at ten times aphid speed, Anna whizzed through the cosmos.

WHEEEEE!

Anna whirled around at a dizzying speed. When she finally let go, she couldn't fly in a straight line but zigzagged around for a bit.

At least three half-eternities later she arrived at a red planet. It was huge. Shaggy red plants grew all over it.

"A forest, almost like the one at home, only not green," rejoiced Anna.

But watch out, Anna! There are many dangers for tiny aphids out in the universe.

All at once, an indescribable roar filled the air. A big black hole darkened the sky and swallowed everything that was not stuck fast to the ground.

Anna grabbed a leaf and held on for dear life.

But skinny little aphid arms are not terribly strong.

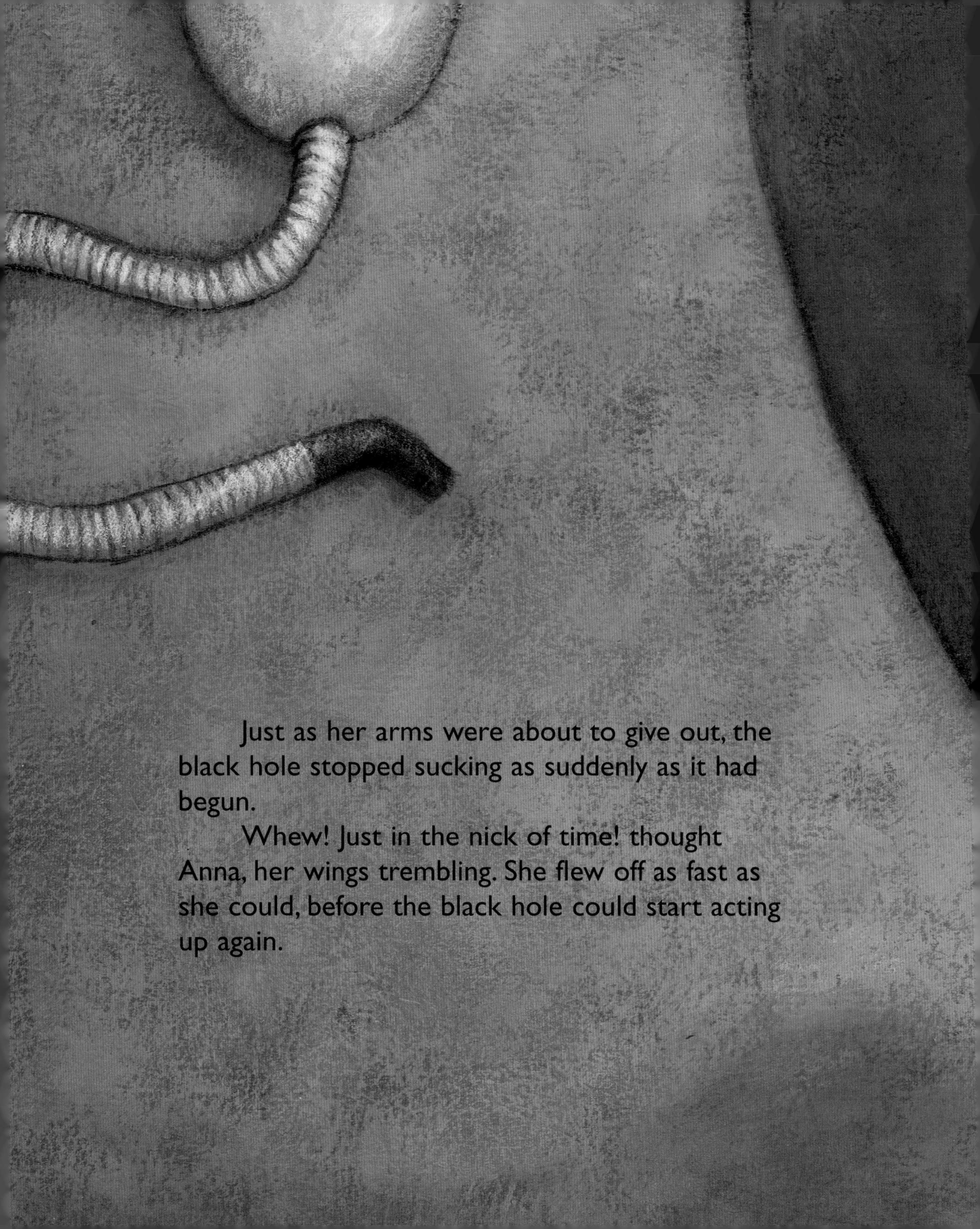

Just as her arms were about to give out, the black hole stopped sucking as suddenly as it had begun.

Whew! Just in the nick of time! thought Anna, her wings trembling. She flew off as fast as she could, before the black hole could start acting up again.

But black holes are not the only danger in the universe. A planet exploded with a loud BANG! The force threw Anna into the air at a hundred times aphid speed.

Helpless, she rocketed through space, until SPLASH! she landed in a bubbling sea.

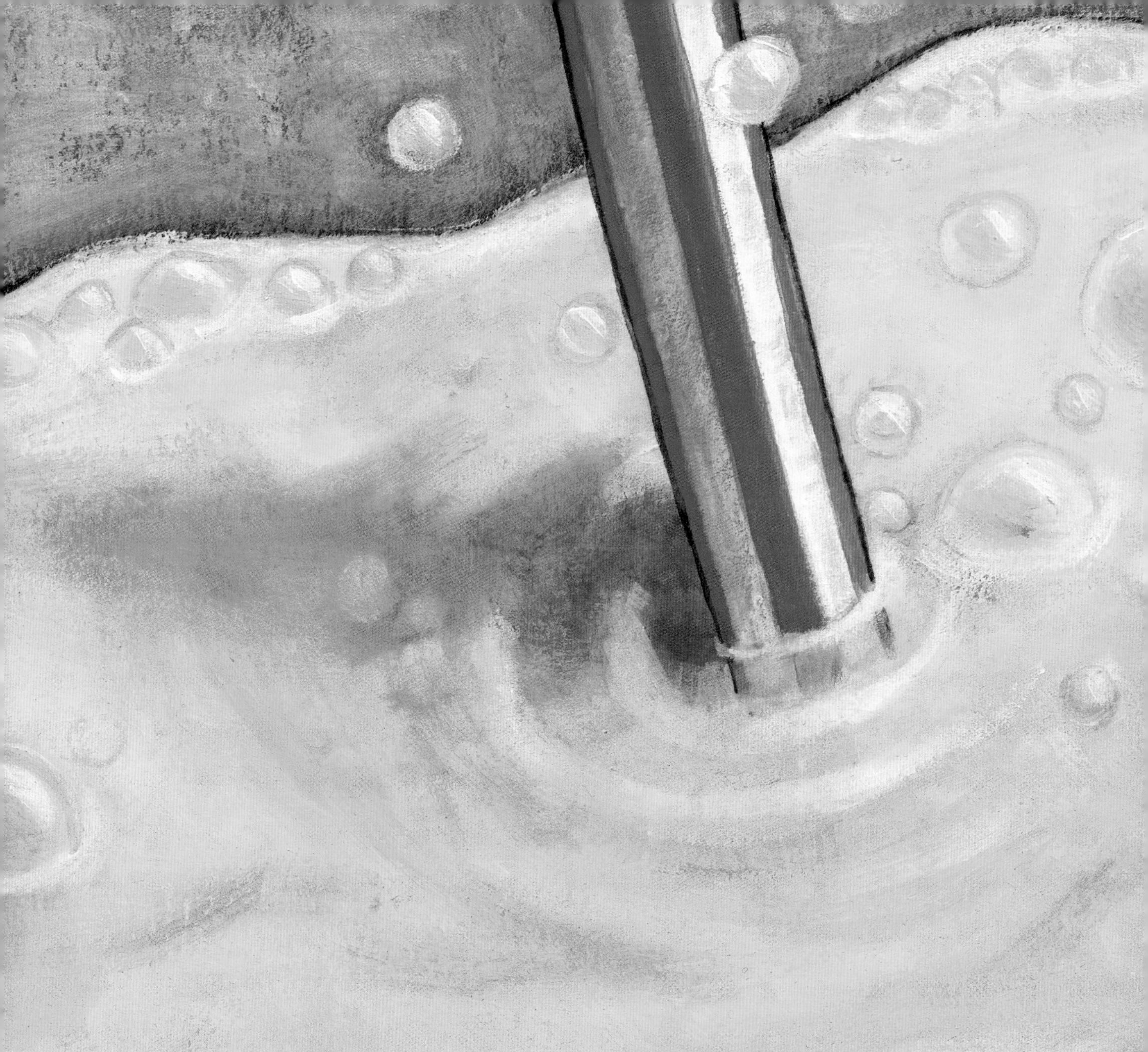

Gasping, she paddled for her life.

At least she didn't go under.

Thank goodness there was some solid land on this planet. With the last of her strength, Anna crawled onto a little island. She was safe. Lucky again, little aphid.

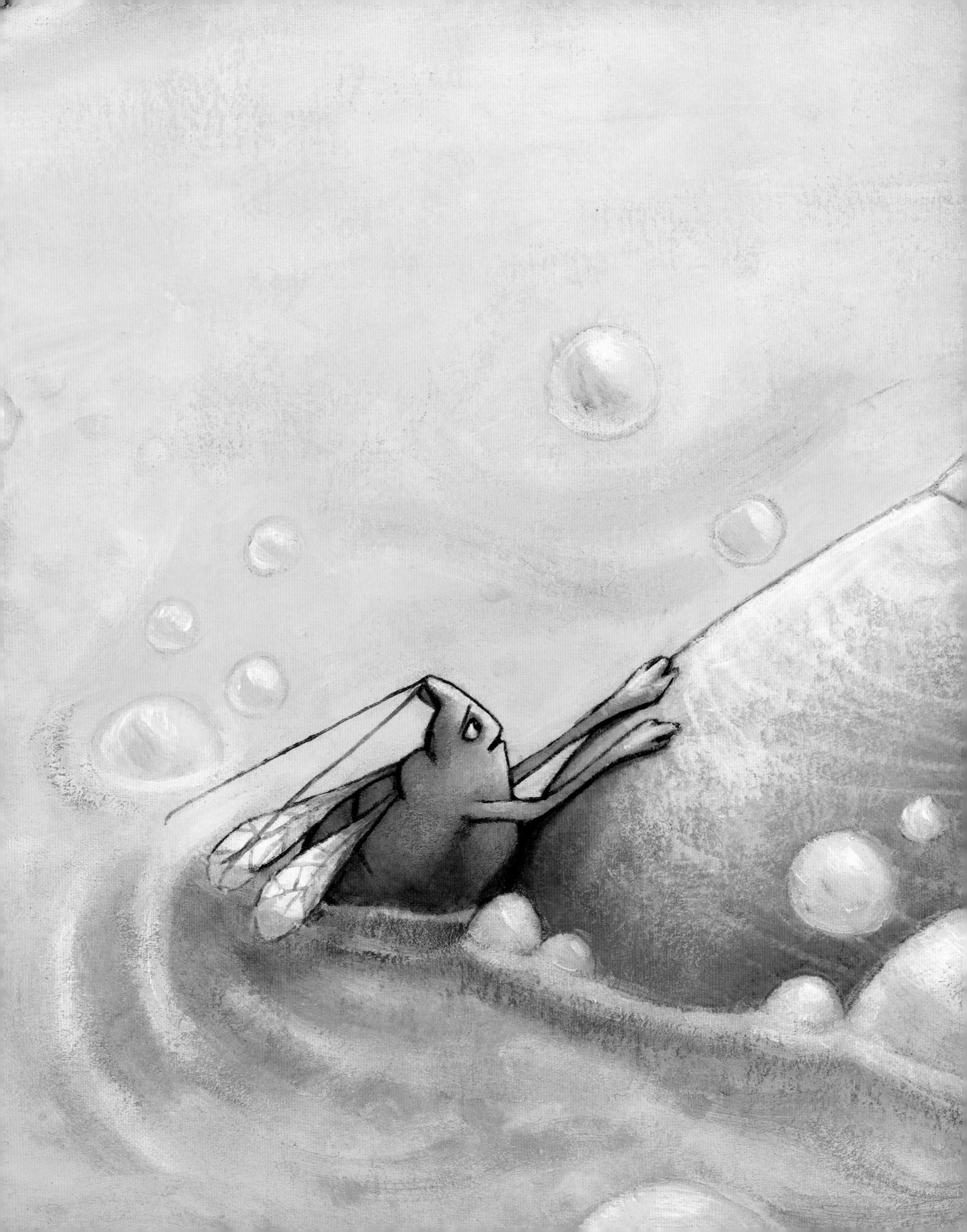

A gentle wind started to blow. It dried Anna's wet wings. The wind was warm, and Anna felt wonderfully safe and secure. Tired, she closed her eyes and took a rest.

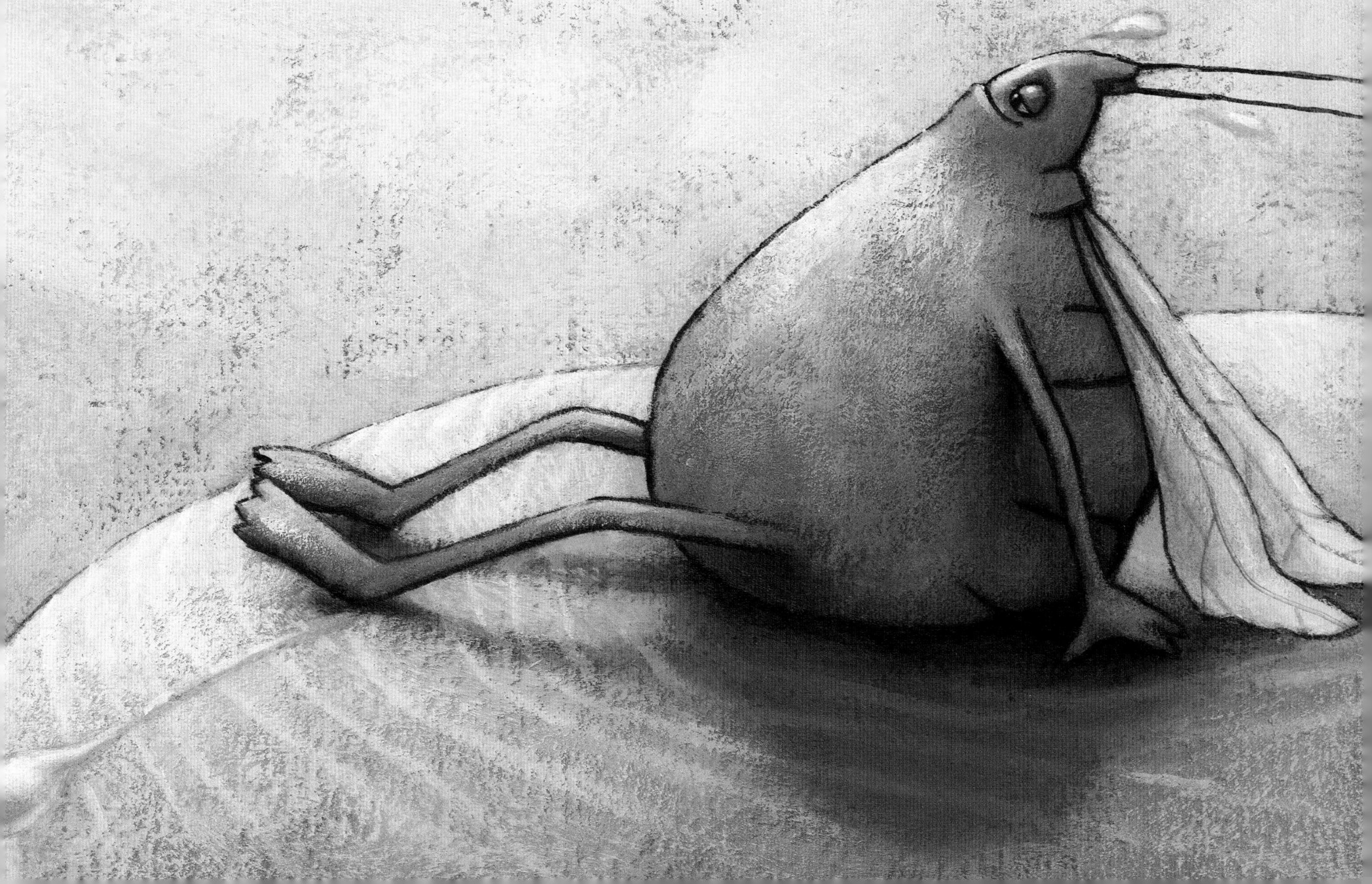

It was time to fly back home. Anna had had enough cosmic adventures for one day.

She spread her wings and let the gentle wind carry her up into the sky.

For what seemed like an eternity, Anna flew through the emptiness of the universe, until she saw the lush green of her planet getting closer.

The whole family had gathered for Anna's return.

"Tell us what you've seen! What lies beyond the end of the world?" her siblings asked excitedly.

"The edge of our planet is not the end at all," Anna said. "It is just the beginning."

Then she told them about all the amazing things that she had seen on her journey.

"What about other aphids? Did you see any?" Papa asked.

"No," answered Anna. "I didn't meet any other forms of intelligent life. But the universe is so big! Who knows what is out there waiting for us."